Bea and Brodies' MAGICAL JOURNEY

featuring the art of Heather McLennan

and

the words of Susan Cohen

First edition, 2021
The Wee Book Company Ltd

The Wee Book Company

www.theweebookcompany.com

Art/illustration copyright ©Heather McLennan
Text copyright ©Susan Cohen

A catalogue record of this book is available from the British Library.

ISBN 9781913237295

Graphic design consultancy by www.colorprinz.com
Printed in Scotland by Bell & Bain Ltd, Glasgow

Brodie woke one morning
And through his sleepy eyes
He saw a wee thing whizzing by
Was it a horsefly?

He wasn't very sure
It wasn't very clear
Could a pesky beastie
Be buzzing oh so near?

He glanced at his pal, Kelpie
Who grazed quietly nearby
Kelpie was so still and calm
Brodie wondered why?

For Kelpie was a blazing boy
Who'd run wild with the herd
If he'd seen a horsefly near
He surely would have stirred?

KICKS

Brodie was so puzzled
He was in an awfy muddle
In the wee blink of an eye
His mind got him into trouble!

He started getting angry
Highland cows and flies don't mix!
He started running round his field
Bucking double back hoof k-i-c-k-s!

'Brodie!' cried Bea, his dearest friend
A light-hearted honey bee
'Whatever is the matter?
Whatever can it be?'

'I think I've seen a horsefly
Maybe more than one
I'm trying to escape them
By going on the run!'

Brodie leapt across the wall
And caused a great commotion
As if there was a farmyard quake
A big bovine explosion!

Mac and Harris yelped and yowled
The herd just stood and stared
As Brodie sent three milking pails
Flying through the air!

Bea buzzed to her big friend's side
Why the agitation?
The air around was clean and clear
Flies were in his imagination!

'Dear Brodie, please don't get upset
There's really nothing there
Your mind is playing tricks on you
It's giving you a scare!

Just you take some big deep breaths
To calm yourself right down
Then use your new found calmness
To turn this great day round!'

One thing Brodie knew for sure
Was that his wee Bea was flighty -
She may be teeny tiny
But her wisdom, it was mighty!

Our minds make our lives magic
If we keep them calm
Let's focus only on the good
That works just like a charm

For magic is a million things
To sense it is a choice
If we keep calm, clear and still
It won't be drowned out by life's noise.

It's in the music through the darkness
It's in the chimes of ancient clocks
It's in the dancing of the moonlight
It's in a castle built on rock

It's in our beloved Scotland
A land with magic in its air
With magic in its soil, its water
Celtic magic everywhere!

The friends journeyed North to Orkney
To its legendary islands
Imagined by the wild blue ocean
Rocks shining bright like diamonds.

The isle of HetherBlether
Is said to rise up through the mist
The home of magic Finfolk
Where green hills gently kiss

The low dark Northern clouds
Then the isle's said to sink away
Letting Bea and Brodie wish
They could just do that some days.

They would like to disappear
Whenever they decide
Where would you just vanish to,
To cast your cares aside?

The friends went next to Moray
To a rose-coloured namesake
To historic Brodie Castle
Where they did a double-take

As romping in the gardens
Through the trees, across the lawn
Was a majestic creature
A magic unicorn!

Full of strength and light and love
Wild, untamed and proud
Through the peaceful silence
They heard it clear and loud

'There is magic everywhere
You must take time to see
The heart is wiser than the mind
Just trust and let it be!'

Then they travelled Southwards
Where Mother Nature casts
Her magic spell of wonder
Which lifts our hearts and lasts

Throughout each of the seasons
Ever-changing every day
Giving our lives energy
In her all-powerful way.

In stunning Dawyck Gardens
The friends stood and gave her thanks
For her bounty and her beauty
Surrounded by her living plants

Who spoke in sweet green voices
'Let our Mother bring you peace
Through us she gives her great magic
To the earth, her masterpiece.'

Bea and Brodie headed homewards
Full of energy, so strong
Grateful to have glimpsed into
Worlds which secretly belong

To Mother Nature, sprites and fairies
Mermaids, monsters in the deep
Myths and legends full of magic
That we can tap into and keep

Safely in our hearts
Which can get tired by wordly cares
We all need a little magic
But now we know it's there

Let's keep our eyes wide open
Let's look for tiny signs
Of magic which surrounds us
It's what makes our lives divine!

Be with those who let us clearly see
The magic in ourselves
Their love floods us with warm bright light
Which magically dispells

Any clouds of darkness
Which hang over our heads
So be like Bea and Brodie
For they once wisely said

You can make each day a good day
It's all up to YOU
Open up to life's great magic
YOU can make your dreams come true!

Then make your way back home
A place where love lives in your heart
Where your feet are firmly on the ground
Eyes lifted to the stars.

You were born with a strong mind
Which can make your life great
In this ever-changing world
You have the power to create

Magic of your own
Wherever you may be
Be calm and use your mighty mind
Magic's there ... you'll see ... you'll see ...

To purchase prints of illustrations appearing in this book and keep up with the latest adventures of Bea and Brodie, go to www.theweebookcompany.com

A donation is made to It's Good 2 Give from every book sale. This wonderful charity supports young cancer patients and their families through difficult times, and provides them with much-needed periods of respite and relaxation at its award-winning Ripple Retreat on beautiful Loch Venachar.

More information about the charity can be found at www.itsgood2give.co.uk